# Karen's in Love

**Here are some other books
about Karen
that you might enjoy:**

## Little Sister

# Karen's in Love

## Ann M. Martin

Illustrations by Susan Tang

A
**LITTLE APPLE**
PAPERBACK

SCHOLASTIC INC.
New York Toronto London Auckland Sydney

*For Barbara, Michael, and Lucy*

ISBN 0-590-43645-7

12 11 10 9 8 7 6 5 4 3 2 1            1 2 3 4 5 6/9

Printed in the U.S.A.        40

First Scholastic printing, February 1991

# 1

## Pamela's Presents

"Thank you, Mrs. Dawes! 'Bye, Nancy. I'll see you in school tomorrow!"

Nancy Dawes is one of my best friends. (I have two.) We are both seven. We are in Ms. Colman's second-grade class at Stoney-brook Academy. Mrs. Dawes had just driven me home from school and dropped me off in front of my mother's house. (Nancy lives next door to me.)

I ran across our lawn and through our front door. Usually I yell, "Hello! I'm home!" and then I look for Mommy and Andrew.

1

Andrew is my little brother. He is four, going on five.

But today I had just opened the door when Andrew ran to meet me.

"Karen! Karen!" he cried. "You got mail today!"

Mail! Wow. I hardly ever get mail. Most of our mail is for Mommy. Or else it is junk mail, and Mommy throws it away.

"Where? Where's my mail?" I cried. I dropped my book bag on the floor. I did not even bother to take off my winter coat or my scarf. I did take off my mittens, though. If I did not do that, how could I open the envelope?

"It's in the kitchen," Andrew answered. He ran in ahead of me. Then he ran back out, carrying the mail. We crashed into each other.

"OW!" we said, but we did not mind the crash. Andrew handed me an envelope. He waited while I tore into it.

"Ooh, it's a birthday invitation," I said.

"Someone is having a party." I opened the card.

"Oh, no!" I cried.

"What?" asked Andrew. He leaned over to look at the card. I do not know why. He can't read yet.

"It's an invitation to *Pamela Harding's* birthday party." I can't stand Pamela. Or her friends Jannie and Leslie. And they can't stand Nancy or Hannie or me. (Hannie is my other best friend. She lives near Daddy's house. She is also in Ms. Colman's class. She and Nancy and I call ourselves the Three Musketeers.)

"I wonder if Nancy and Hannie got invited to Pamela's party, too," I said.

I dashed into the kitchen. "Hi, Mommy! School was fine. I need to use the phone," I cried. Then I thought of something. "Can I use the phone in your bedroom? I think I am going to need privacy."

Mommy said I could use her phone, so I ran upstairs. I called Nancy.

"Hi, Nancy?" I said. "Did you get an invitation to — "

" — Pamela's birthday party?" Nancy finished for me. "Yeah. . . . Darn it."

"Now we have to get her presents," I said. "Who wants to get presents for Pamela, anyway? She'll hate whatever we buy her."

"Let's get her things she won't want," suggested Nancy.

"Yeah. She'll have to pre*tend* she likes them. We could get her really yucky things or really mean things."

"Like the prize in a Cracker Jacks box?" said Nancy.

I giggled.

Nancy and Hannie and I called each other all afternoon. We had different ideas about what presents we should get for Pamela.

Nancy stuck to her Cracker Jacks prize. But I think she was kidding. Her mother would never let her take a Cracker Jacks prize to a birthday party.

Hannie wanted to get her something babyish, like pink mittens, with clips to fasten them to the sleeves of her ski jacket.

I did not know what to get her . . . yet. But I would think of something.

# Two Families

I bet you're wondering something. I bet you're wondering why my mommy has one house and my daddy has another house.

Well, that is because my parents are divorced. They used to be married. That was a long time ago — when they had Andrew and me. They loved each other then. But after awhile they decided they did not love each other anymore. They loved Andrew and me, but not each other. So they got divorced. Daddy stayed in that big house. He had grown up in the house. But Mommy moved to a little house. She took Andrew and me with her. Luckily, the big house and the little house are in the same town — Stoneybrook, Connecticut.

Guess what. A couple of years after Mommy and Daddy got divorced, they each got married again. Mommy married a man named Seth. He's my stepfather. When Seth moved into our house, he brought his cat and dog with him. His cat's name is Rocky and his dog's name is Midgie. I like animals, and I like Rocky and Midgie a lot. But not their names. I would have chosen better names for them. Oh, there is another pet at our house. It is my rat. Her name is Emily Junior.

Andrew and I live with Mommy and Seth most of the time. But every other weekend, and for two weeks in the summer, we live with Daddy at the big house. Boy. You would not believe all the people who live there. It is a good thing the house is so big.

At Daddy's house are Daddy, of course, and his wife. His wife's name is Elizabeth.

She is my stepmother. Elizabeth has *four* kids! Three boys and a girl. Sam and Charlie are in high school. I like having big brothers, but Sam teases me. David Michael is my age, but he does not go to my school. David Michael is okay. He calls me Professor sometimes because I wear glasses. I even have two pairs of glasses. One is for reading. The other is for the rest of the time. (By the way, "Professor" is a nice nickname, not a mean one.) Anyway, then there is my stepsister, Kristy. I love Kristy so, so much. She is one of my favorite people in the whole wide world. Kristy is thirteen. She baby-sits.

There are still *more* people at the big house. There is Emily Michelle. She is two and a half. Emily is adopted. She came from a country called Vietnam. That is far away. (I named Emily, my rat, after her.) Finally, there is Nannie. Nannie is Elizabeth's mother. That means she is my stepgrandmother. Nannie takes care of Emily while Daddy and Elizabeth are at work and everyone else is at school. There are also two animals at the big house. One is Shannon, David Michael's puppy. The other is Boo-Boo. He is Daddy's fat, old mean cat. I usually try to stay away from Boo-Boo.

You know what? I call my brother Andrew Two-Two and I call myself Karen Two-Two. (I got the names from a book Ms. Colman read to our class. It was called *Jacob Two-Two Meets the Hooded Fang*.) Andrew and I are two-twos because we have two mommies, two daddies, two families, two cats, two dogs, two houses, and more.

I have two best friends. Andrew and I each have toys and clothes and books at the big house and at the little house. I have a bicycle at each house and Andrew has a tricycle at each house. I even have two stuffed cats that are just the same. Moosie stays at the big house, Goosie stays at the little house. Having two of so many things is helpful because it means that Andrew and I don't have to pack much when we go from one house to the other.

Being a two-two might sound like fun.

Most of the time it is. But some things are not fun. I miss my rat when I go to the big house. And I did not have two special blankets. My blanket is named Tickly. For a long time, there was only one Tickly. I kept leaving Tickly behind at the big house or the little house. Finally I ripped Tickly in half so that I could have two pieces. I hope I did not hurt Tickly.

Let's see. A few more things. I have blonde hair and blue eyes. I have some freckles, too. Once, I broke my wrist roller-skating. So that's me, Karen Two-Two Brewer. My life is *almost* perfect.

If I could just figure out what to get Pamela for her dumb old birthday party. . . .

# 3

# Jinx on Pamela

The day after I got the invitation to Pamela's party was another school day. Hannie and Nancy and Ricky Torres and I arrived at school early. We got to our classroom even before Ms. Colman. So did a bunch of other kids. But not Pamela. She had not come in yet.

"You want to hear something weird?" Ricky said. (Ricky has asked me to marry him. We will be planning a wedding soon. I think I love Ricky.)

"I always want to hear weird things," I told Ricky.

"Yeah," agreed Nancy, Hannie, Natalie Springer, and two boys.

"I got an invitation to Pamela Harding's birthday party," said Ricky.

"Me, too," said everyone else.

"What's she doing inviting *boys* to her party?" asked Bobby Gianelli. "I don't want to go to some girlie party."

"Well, what's she doing inviting *us*?" asked Natalie. (She meant herself and Hannie and Nancy and me.) "She doesn't like us."

"I wonder why we were all invited," I said aloud.

"Because my parents *made* me invite you," a voice replied.

I whirled around. There stood Pamela. Leslie and Jannie were with her. They are always together, and they are almost always mean.

"My parents," Pamela went on, "said I

had to invite everyone in my class. They said that was the only fair thing to do. Especially since I am new here."

Pamela joined our class after school began. Her family had just moved to Stoneybrook. At first, we were very interested in Pamela. She wears *cool* clothes. And her father is a dentist, and her mother writes books. Plus, she has a sister who is sixteen and lets Pamela wear her *perfume*. We all (well, all the girls) wanted Pamela to be our friend. But then we found out how snobby she is.

She proved it again right then. "*I* wish I could have had a sleepover just for my *special* friends," she said. She glanced at Leslie and Jannie. The three of them smiled.

"I wish you could have, too," I told her.

Pamela made a face at me. Then she and Leslie and Jannie went to a corner of the room to talk by themselves.

"Boo," I said to Ricky. "I know my mother will make me go to the party."

"So will mine," said Ricky.

"Hey! Maybe we can jinx Pamela's party," I exclaimed. Then I lowered my voice. "You know, we can play tricks and stuff."

"Yeah!" whispered Ricky. "We can tell Pamela things. Like . . . like I found a spider in my piece of cake and now I am going to barf."

I laughed. "If we play Pin-the-Tail-on-the-Donkey, we should try to tape the tail on Pamela instead!"

"We can bring Pamela presents that look beautiful. But when she unwraps them, the boxes will be empty," said Hannie.

"Oh!" I said to Ricky. "Hannie and Nancy and I talked about presents yesterday. We decided to bring baby stuff, or things Pamela won't like."

"Good idea," said Ricky. "I will do that, too. What are you going to bring, Karen?"

"I haven't decided yet. It has to be just the wrong thing."

Ricky smiled. "Let's see. I could bring her a snake."

"A *real* one?" I shuddered.

"Well, I was thinking of a rubber one. But a real snake would be even better. I wonder where I can get one."

Ricky and I could not stop laughing. We were imagining Pamela opening a box — and finding a snake inside!

# 4

# Valentine's Day

*C*lap, *clap, clap.*

Ms. Colman was standing in front of her desk. She was ready to start class. She wanted to get our attention.

Everyone ran for their desks. We like Ms. Colman a lot. We try to please her. (At least, I do.)

Hannie and Nancy ran to the back of the room. They sit next to each other in the last row.

Ricky and I ran to the front of the room. We sit next to each other in the first row.

17

That is because we both wear glasses. (So does Natalie Springer. She sits on the other side of Ricky.) I used to sit in the back with Hannie and Nancy. That was before I got my glasses.

Ms. Colman is a patient teacher. She hardly *ever* yells. And she is nice when she has to remind me about things. See, I am the youngest one in our class. (That is because I skipped from kindergarten to first grade in the middle of school last year.) Sometimes I forget to wear my glasses. Ms. Colman reminds me nicely. Sometimes I forget to raise my hand in class. Ms. Colman reminds me not to call out. And sometimes I forget to use my quiet voice in the classroom. Then Ms. Colman just says, "Indoor voice, please, Karen." Ms. Colman is my best teacher ever.

"Okay, class," said Ms. Colman when we were sitting down. "I have an announcement to make."

I grinned and sneaked a peek back at

Hannie and Nancy. We love Ms. Colman's Surprising Announcements.

"Girls and boys," Ms. Colman went on, "as you know, Valentine's Day is coming up." (Yea! I *adore* holidays. I try to celebrate every one, even the small ones like Arbor Day. Plus, last December, I celebrated Christmas with my family, and Hanukkah with Nancy's family. Now it was time for cards and candy and hearts and maybe little presents.) "How would you like to celebrate Valentine's Day?" Ms. Colman asked us.

She was leaving it up to us? Wow!

"A party!" cried Nancy.

"Yeah!" said just about everyone, even Pamela.

"That would be gigundo fun," I added.

"I," said Terri, who has a twin sister, "would like to take a trip to the aquarium."

"Me, too," said Tammy. (Tammy is Terri's twin.)

"No!" shouted the rest of us.

"Hold on," said Ms. Colman. "What happened to raising your hands?" Then she went on, "I think we'll be having a party. What will we do at our party?"

Bobby raised his hand. "Eat," he said. "Can we have cupcakes and candy?"

"I think so," replied Ms. Colman. "What else?"

"Play games," said Hannie, who remembered to raise her hand, too.

Then Natalie raised *her* hand.

"Yes, Natalie?" said Ms. Colman.

"We'll give each other valentines, won't we?"

"Of course. We will each make our own mailbox."

That made me think of something. I would give Ricky a valentine surprise. But what? A gift? It would have to be something special. Extra-super-gigundo special. After all, Ricky and I were engaged.

So what could I get him for Valentine's Day? A bow tie? No, that would be boring. Candy? Maybe, but that was not very special.

Now I had to think of *two* presents to give to people. A yucky one for Pamela and a nice one for Ricky.

# 5

# Pamela's Party

One Saturday I woke up at the little house. The first thing I did was groan. That was not because I had a stomachache.

It was because it was the day of Pamela Harding's birthday party. Oh, well. At least I was not the only one who did not want to go.

I had finally found a present for Pamela. It was a package with five plastic bracelets in it: pink, blue, green, yellow, and purple. I knew that Pamela would not like them. I was not even sure they would fit her.

"Is this *really* what you want to take to Pamela's party?" Mommy asked me when we were in the store. "We could get something else. Or we could get something to go with the bracelets. Maybe a locket?"

"Nope. The bracelets are fine," I told Mommy. "They're perfect for Pamela." I took them home and wrapped them up. I wrapped them sloppily.

On the day of the party, I did not get dressed up. I just put on a pair of jeans and a baggy red sweater. I thought about wearing my party shoes. I wore my sneakers instead. Then I looked at my hair ribbons and barrettes. I did not put any on.

"Is that how you're going to Pamela's party?" Mommy asked when she saw me.

"Yup," I replied.

Mommy shrugged. "Okay."

Mommy drove Nancy and Hannie and me to Pamela's house. Nancy had not been allowed to give Pamela a Cracker Jacks prize. Her parents made her buy a game. Hannie

23

had not been allowed to give Pamela the baby mittens. *Her* parents made her buy a pair of gigundo cool pants. They were pink leggings. And they were just Pamela's style.

Oh, well, I thought. Ricky is bringing a live snake.

Mommy dropped us off at Pamela's house and watched to make sure that we got inside okay. We had not been to Pamela's before. When we stepped into her house, it looked like a circus. Balloons and streamers were everywhere. A huge sign said HAPPY BIRTHDAY, PAMELA! A clown was walking around. And someone who was wearing all black clothes was carrying some paints. Everyone except Hannie and Nancy and I was dressed up.

"Hi," said Pamela. "Come on in. This is my circus birthday." Pamela looked very proud of herself.

I was so suprised that I forgot to say, "Happy birthday." So did Hannie and Nancy. We just handed Pamela her presents. Then we took off our coats.

I looked around for Ricky. He was not there yet. Boo.

I looked at the kids in the living room. All the boys were crowded to one side. All the girls were crowded to the other side. The clown was trying to make them talk to each other. He was not having much luck. I felt bad for him.

Soon the doorbell rang again. There were Bobby and . . . Ricky! Ricky's present looked like it was just the right size for a snake.

Since everyone had arrived, Pamela's sister came into the living room. "Let the party begin!" she cried.

What a party it was! The clown turned out to be a juggler. He juggled balls and canes and hats. He balanced a Ping-Pong ball on his nose. The person dressed in black came around and painted our faces. She painted me to look like a cat.

When the juggler and painter were finished, it was time to sit down at the special birthday table. The dining room was decorated to look like a circus wagon. There

were goody bags at each place at the table, and boy, were they fancy. They were made of either red or blue cellophane, and they were tied with gold ribbon.

Pamela's mother and father brought in the birthday cake. We sang "Happy Birthday," and Pamela made a wish before she blew out the candles. I leaned over to look at the cake. It was the fanciest one I had ever seen.

I kept waiting for Ricky to do or say something mean to Pamela. After all, we had agreed to jinx Pamela's party. But Ricky had been . . . well, he had been *nice* to Pamela. He had told her he liked the juggler. He had told her he liked the artist. (The artist made Ricky look like Darth Vader.) He had told Pamela the cake and the goody bags were neat. He had even told her that her dress was pretty.

I was gigundo mad. I did not talk to Ricky. I stuck with Hannie and Nancy.

Oh, well. There was still the snake to look forward to.

# Purple Suspenders

When we had eaten the cake and ice cream, Mrs. Harding said, "Okay, boys and girls. You may now look inside your goody bags."

I wondered if Mrs. Harding always talked like that.

I did not bother to wonder for long, though. Goody bags are exciting. We reached for ours quickly. The blue bags were for the boys. The red bags were for the girls. So I untied the gold string on my red bag. I

reached inside. I could not believe what I found there. In my bag was:

— a page of stickers (fuzzy ones)
— a little clipboard with papers on it (The stationery had rainbows at the top.)
— a pencil with an eraser that looked like a slice of birthday cake
— some candy
— Silly Putty (When I opened the egg I found bright *yellow* Silly Putty.)
— some beads and strings for making jewelry
— a one-dollar bill. That was at the very bottom of the bag. A whole dollar! (The bracelets I was giving Pamela only cost a dollar. Uh-oh. . . .)

In the boys' goody bags were:

— a little paddle ball
— a blow-up plastic crayon (The crayon would get huge!)
— a pocket puzzle

— Silly Putty

— some candy

— a pencil with an eraser that looked like a helicopter

— and a dollar.

Whew! *Nobody* could believe the goody bags. They had more stuff in them than we'd ever seen in any goody bag.

I looked at Ricky, who was across the table from me. Ricky was gawking at all his goody-bag stuff. Then he looked at Pamela. He *smiled* at her.

Now that Pamela had given us presents, it was time for her to open *her* presents. We sat on the floor in the living room. Pamela sat next to the pile of gifts. She began ripping into them. Everyone had brought pretty nice presents — games and toys and things. I began to worry about my bracelets. Maybe I could snatch them away. Maybe Pamela would not notice that I hadn't brought a present.

Too late. Pamela reached for the bracelets

at the same time I did. She took off the wrapping paper. She looked at the plastic bracelets. "Gee, thanks," she said to me. She tossed the package aside. Only Ricky's present was left. I sat up straight.

The snake! Ooh. I bet Pamela would scream.

Pamela unwrapped Ricky's gift. I wriggled with excitement. She lifted the lid off of the box. Inside was . . . a pair of purple suspenders.

"Ricky!" cried Pamela. "These are great! I can wear them with my blue pants."

Ricky grinned. Pamela grinned back.

I nudged Ricky in the ribs. "I thought you were getting her a snake," I whispered.

"My mother wouldn't let me," Ricky whispered back.

"Traitor," I muttered. I did not believe him. "Why did you have to get her something so nice?"

Ricky just shrugged.

Ooh. Boo.

By the time the party was over, I felt

terrible. I was the only one who had given Pamela an awful gift. In return, I had gotten a wonderful goody bag, a silver balloon (it was tied to the back of my chair — we all got one), and some yummy cake. Plus I had seen a juggler and had my face made up like a cat.

I was a terrible person.

Well, not really. But I felt like one that day.

# 7

# Ricky and Karen

"Hi, Karen!"

That was Ricky. It was the Monday after Pamela's birthday party. My classmates and I were gathering in Ms. Colman's room.

I heard Ricky, but I did not answer him. I had decided he liked Pamela better than he liked me. He had a crush on Pamela.

"Karen? Hi," Ricky tried again.

I turned to Nancy. "Andrew learned to add up the dots on dice yesterday," I told her. "We were playing a board game. He is really smart."

*"Karen,"* said Ricky. "Did you hear me? Why won't you answer me?"

Hannie and Nancy looked at Ricky and me. They knew why I was not answering. They knew that I was mad at Ricky. But they did not want to join the fight.

I sat down at my desk.

"Hello, boys and girls," said Ms. Colman's voice.

It was time to begin our day. I was saved.

Ricky sat at his desk, too. I could tell he was puzzled.

Later that morning, Ms. Colman gave us spelling words. When we were finished she said, "Okay. Please switch papers with a neighbor. Check each other's spelling."

Ricky and I usually switch. So Ricky passed his paper to me. But *I* passed *my* paper to the kid behind me. "I am not talking to you, Ricky," I said.

"You are right now," he pointed out.

I ignored what he said.

"You're a traitor," I told him. "You did not do one mean thing to Pamela at her

35

party. You promised you would. But you were *nice* to Pamela. You didn't even give her a snake."

Ricky snatched his paper off of my desk, He passed it to Natalie Springer.

"So what?" was all Ricky replied.

On the playground that afternoon, Ricky said, "Come on, Karen. Play dodgeball with us, okay? We need another player."

Of course I did not answer Ricky. Ricky looked surprised. Then he looked hurt.

After recess, Ms. Colman said, "Time to choose partners again. I want you to work together to write a poem. Working together to make something is called 'collaboration.' And you need to cooperate. Your poem does not have to be long, and it does not have to rhyme. You have fifteen minutes to work."

I turned away from Ricky again. He could work with Natalie for the rest of the year. I did not care. But guess what. I heard Ricky say, "Pamela? Want to work with me? I have a good idea for a poem."

I jerked my head around. Ricky was looking at me. He smiled.

And Pamela answered, "Sure, Ricky."

So. Ricky *did* have a crush on Pamela.

My partner and I wrote our poem. We finished early. Then I wrote another poem by myself. It went like this: "To Yicky Ricky from Karen. Ricky and Pamela sitting in a tree. K-I-S-S-I-N-G. First comes love, then comes marriage, then comes Pamela with a baby carriage."

I folded the note in half and left it on Ricky's desk.

When our fifteen minutes were over, Ricky went back to his desk.

He saw the note.

He opened it up.

Then he turned to me and stuck out his tongue.

I stuck out my tongue at Ricky.

So Ricky wadded up the note into a tiny

ball. Then he put it into his mouth. Ew. Now it was a *spit*ball.

Ricky threw it at me when Ms. Colman was not looking.

I had a feeling that Ricky and I might not get married after all.

8

# Hearts and Flowers

I knew just how to cure the Wedding Blues. (That was Kristy's name for the way I was feeling about Ricky.) I would cure the Wedding Blues by making valentines for the people in my two families. I would help Andrew make his, too.

One afternoon at the little house, I got out red and white construction paper. I found a package of doilies. Then I found cotton balls and yarn and glitter and scissors and glue. Mommy spread newspapers on the kitchen table.

"Go to town!" she said.

"To town?" repeated Andrew.

"She means have fun," I told him.

And we did. First I started by making a regular valentine. I cut out a red heart. Then I got an idea.

"Mommy?" I said. "Do we have any old magazines? Ones that we're going to recycle?"

"Yup," said Mommy. She brought us a stack of them.

"Oh, goody! Thank you," I said.

I found pictures of flowers in one magazine. I cut them out. I glued them around the edge of the heart.

In the middle of the heart I wrote: "Sam, Sam, Sam. The love of my heart. I hope that we will never part." I knew Sam would think the poem was funny.

"Karen, help me," said Andrew then. "I can't make a heart." He held up what he had just cut out of a piece of red paper. This is what it looked like:

"That isn't bad, Andrew," I said. But I did help him make a better heart.

"I can't wait for Valentine's Day," said Andrew.

"Me, neither," I replied. "And remember. We get two Valentine's Day celebrations with our families. On the real Valentine's Day, we will have a special breakfast here at the little house. Then that night we go to Daddy's. And the next day we have a party at the big house."

"Yup," said Andrew happily. He had just cut out a very good heart.

I wrote another poem: "Roses are red. Grass is green. I love you, David Michael, even when you're mean."

Already I felt better.

## 9

# Picky, Yicky, Sticky Ricky

Maybe I felt better at home. But I did not feel better at school.

When Ricky and I first started our fight, we were the only ones fighting. Nobody else wanted to be part of it.

Ricky and I thought up all sorts of mean things to do to each other. And Ricky did the first mean thing. He was the one who brought ink to school with him. He spilled it all over a picture I was coloring one morning.

"Oops," said Ricky. "Sorry. It was an accident." He smiled at me.

"Was not!" I cried.

"Oh, well."

So later on in the day, I did something I *really* should not have done. I chewed up a piece of gum. Then I stretched it out and stuck it around in Ricky's desk. That was bad enough. But here is the worst thing. Ms. Colman says we cannot have gum in school. But I had a piece anyway, *and* I chewed it, *and* I messed up Ricky's desk. I did it while he was in the bathroom. Ms. Colman did not see. She was busy helping Bobby Gianelli with something.

When Ricky came back, the first thing he did was reach into his desk. I think he was looking for his math book. When he pulled his hand out, long strings of gum came with it.

I wish I had had a camera so I could have taken a picture of the look on Ricky's face when he saw the gum gooing away from

the inside of his desk. First he looked surprised. Then he just looked disgusted.

"Gross!" he said, but not too loudly. We
both knew that we did not want Ms. Colman
to see what was going on. We would not
tattle on each other. Our fight was private.

Ricky put his hand back into his desk.
Then he pulled it out again.

More gum.

Ricky glared at me. "Karen — "he started
to say.

"Oops," I interrupted him. "Sorry. It was
an accident." I smiled at Ricky.

"Was not. You did that on purpose. Gum
doesn't accidentally get — "

He stopped talking. Ms. Colman had left
Bobby. She was heading for her desk.

Ricky tried to rub the gum off of his hand
before Ms. Colman saw it. He was lucky.
He got it all off. But later, it took him forever
to clean out his desk.

"Picky, yicky, sticky Ricky," I whispered
to him.

"Rotten Karen," was all Ricky could think of to say.

"That doesn't rhyme," I told him flatly.

The next day, Ricky mashed a banana inside *my* desk. Then Hannie and Nancy got mad. They started calling Ricky "Sticky Ricky," because of the gum.

The boys joined the fight. They were on Ricky's side, of course. The boys did not have a good nickname for me. They were too dumb to think of one.

Guess who else joined Ricky's side. Pamela, Jannie, and Leslie.

When we were on the playground one day, Nancy and Hannie and I stood in a row. We linked our arms. We sang, *"Sticky Ricky! Sticky Ricky! Picky, yicky, sticky Ricky!"* Then we stuck out our tongues at him.

Ricky was playing catch with Bobby and Hank. The boys stopped when they heard our song. They turned to look at us. So did Pamela and Jannie and Leslie.

"Four-eyes!" Ricky yelled at me.

"You're a four-eyes, too!" I called back.

"Well, *I'm* not," said Pamela. *"Four-eyes! Four-eyes! Karen is a four-eyes!"*

It was not a good week at Stoneybrook Academy.

I was very glad when it was over.

## 10

# Ricky's Card

After that awful week with Ricky, I decided something. I decided I did not want to be mad at him anymore. But I could not just give up. And I could not apologize to him. Sometimes Daddy calls me a fighter. He does not mean that I hit people. He means that I do not quit easily.

Still, I wanted to quit the fight with Ricky. I wanted to be friends with him. We used to be friends, and that was nice.

Plus, we were engaged.

And Valentine's Day was coming up.

"Valentine's Day would be a good time to make up," Hannie told me. Hannie should know. She's already married. She's married to Scott Hsu. (Scott does not go to our school.)

"That's true," I said. "Anyway, I want to get a valentine from Ricky. I mean, after all, I *like* him, even if we are fighting." (And maybe I love him, I thought.) "So, I just have to figure out a way to make up with him."

"Yeah," agreed Hannie. "That's always the hard part."

One day, Mommy picked me up from school. Andrew was with her.

"Guess what," said Andrew, as soon as I opened the car door.

"What?" I asked.

"*Guess.*"

"I can't."

"Mommy is taking us to town. We're going to buy Valentine's Day cards."

"I thought that you and Andrew," said

51

Mommy, "would like to *buy* cards to give to your friends. You already worked so hard making your other cards."

"Goody!" I exclaimed. "I want those cards with jokes and riddles on them."

"I want animal valentines," said Andrew.

Mommy took us to the dime store. (Almost nothing in there costs a dime, so it's a silly name.) Andrew and I chose our valentines quickly. We could hardly wait to get home and start signing them.

When we did get home, Mommy found pencils and crayons for us. Andrew and I sat at the kitchen table. We spread out our valentines.

"I'm going to give this kitten to Mandy," said Andrew. He smiled to himself.

*"Andrew has a girlfriend! Andrew has a girlfriend!"* I sang.

Andrew did not pay attention to me. So I figured he really did have a girlfriend.

I got to work on my own valentines. I chose each one very carefully. For Hannie and Nancy, I chose funny jokes that I knew they would like.

Then I chose cards for Natalie and Hank, for the twins, and for everyone I wanted to give cards to — except Ricky. I looked over the cards that were left. None of them seemed quite right for him. And none of them were special.

I remembered that I had thought of getting a present for Ricky. I did not think I should do that now. But maybe I could make him a *really special* card.

So that is what I did. I got out all our supplies again — the red and white paper, the glitter, and even some lace. I cut out a huge heart. I glued lace around the edges. Then I decided that I should write the valentine message in glitter.

But what should I write? I *wanted* to write: "I Love You, Ricky." I did not think that would be a good idea, though. Pamela would laugh. So would a lot of other kids. Finally I just wrote: "To Ricky. Love, Karen."

I was still taking a chance. Pamela might laugh at the word "love." And, if Ricky were mad enough, he might laugh, too.

I hoped I would not get embarrassed at our class party.

# 11

# U R 4 Me

Valentine's Day!

Hurray! Gigundo hurray! Another holiday.

Mommy and Seth fixed a very fancy Valentine's Day breakfast for our little-house family. And I was dressed in a very fancy way. All in red. I put on a red dress, red tights, red sneakers, red bracelet, and even red stick-on earrings. It was too bad that neither of my pairs of glasses was red.

Anyway, I ran into the kitchen and

shouted, "Good morning! Happy Valentine's Day, everyone!"

"Good morning, rosebud," said Seth.

"Rosebud?!" I repeated.

"Yup. You're all red, like a rosebud."

I giggled. Then I sat down at the table with Andrew.

Here is what we had for breakfast: heart-shaped pancakes (Seth made them), cranberry juice, strawberries, and milk with red food coloring in it. A red-heart breakfast!

The breakfast was like a party. In front of everybody's place was a little basket. The baskets were red (of course) and they were full of candy — chocolate kisses and teeny hearts with messages printed on them. The messages said things like "Luv ya" and "My baby" and "Sweetie-pie."

Andrew's favorite was "U R 4 Me." I thought that was very clever.

After we had eaten breakfast, Seth said, "Okay! Time for presents."

Presents! Yea!

Mommy handed Andrew a little gift. Seth

handed me a little gift. We tore the paper off of them. Andrew got a red Matchbox car. I got a pair of red barrettes.

"Oh, thank you!" we cried.

I put the barrettes in my hair right away. Andrew began vrooming his car along the table. Mommy and Seth let him do that until he ran the car into a glass of juice and knocked it over.

After Andrew had cleaned up his mess, Seth said, "Lisa" (that's Mommy's name), "I have something for you."

Mommy said, "And *I* have something for *you*."

She gave Seth a red flower. I think it was a carnation. Seth gave Mommy a red rose. Then they kissed. Right in front of Andrew and me.

"Ew!" Andrew screeched.

"Gross! Ick!" I cried.

Mommy and Seth laughed. Then Mommy said, "Okay, off to school, Karen." (Andrew goes to preschool. He usually goes in the afternoon.)

58

Suddenly I remembered our class party. I remembered our valentines. I remembered my fancy valentine for Ricky. My stomach began to feel funny.

What would Ricky think of the card?

What would Pamela think of it?

Would Ricky give me a valentine?

Ms. Colman had said we did not have to give valentines to every single person in our class. Some teachers make you do that, you know. I think it is stupid. You are supposed to give valentines to people you like. And I do not like Pamela or Jannie or Leslie. So why should I give them cards?

Seth drove me to school that morning. Boy, was I nervous. And all over one silly valentine.

Love makes you feel weird.

At least, I think it was love that was making me feel weird. It could have been all the candy I ate at breakfast.

## 12

# Special Delivery

Even though we had had our long Valentine's Day breakfast, I still got to school early. In fact, I was the first person in Ms. Colman's room.

Whew.

There was a reason that I wanted to get to school early. I wanted to deliver my valentines in private.

The week before, we had made mailboxes for our desks. At least, Ms. Colman had *called* them mailboxes. But they did not look like any mailboxes I had ever seen.

"Boys and girls," Ms. Colman had said.

Yea! I'd thought. I bet this will be a Surprising Announcement.

I was right.

"Today," Ms. Colman had gone on, "we will make mailboxes for our valentines."

Ms. Colman had handed out oaktag. (I did not know what oaktag is. I found out that it is very stiff paper.) We taped two pieces of oaktag together to make a pouch. Then we wrote our names in the middle of the pouch. And *then* we decorated our mailboxes. I used crayons to make a border all around my name. This is what the border looked like:

I colored the hearts pink and red. I colored the flowers orange and yellow.

The pouches were very pretty, but they did not look like mailboxes.

*   *   *

Anyway, on Valentine's Day, I entered Ms. Colman's room with my cards. I was nervous. My stomach still felt funny.

I hung up my coat. Then I put my spelling book away in my desk. And then I took the valentines out of their bag. There was a small pile of the ones that had come from the store.

And there was Ricky's big, fancy card in the big, fancy envelope I had made for it. I looked at the valentine for a long time. Finally I decided that if I were going to put it in Ricky's mailbox, I better do it right then — before anybody saw me.

My hands shook a little as I opened Ricky's mailbox.

I dropped the card inside.

"Special delivery," I whispered.

Then I began to deliver my other cards. I dropped one in Nancy's box, in Hannie's box, in Natalie's box, and kept on going.

Other kids came into the classroom. They

began to deliver their valentines, too. I did not care if they saw me putting the store-bought cards in my friends' boxes. But I was glad that nobody had seen me drop the special card in Ricky's box.

When I was finished delivering, I sat down at my desk. I had not put a card in Pamela's box or Leslie's box or Jannie's box. That will show them, I thought.

I watched the other kids deliver their valentines. I noticed that lots of kids put cards in Pamela's box. I also noticed that Pamela had only three cards to deliver. Let's see. One for Jannie, one for Leslie, and one for . . . *Ricky?* Oh, no.

Where was Ricky? Had he come in yet? I looked all around the room. There he was. He was putting a card in Hannie's box. (That was okay with me.) Would he put a card in my box? Or maybe he had already put one in, while I was busy watching Pamela. How would I know? Ms. Colman had said we could not look in our mailboxes until the party in the afternoon.

I watched Ricky deliver the rest of his cards.

He did not put one in my box.

I wanted to take mine *out* of his, but I could not figure out how.

# Red Hots

**K**nock, knock, knock.

I looked at the door to our classroom.

The room mothers were here! It was time for our school party to begin.

Usually, I just love parties. I cannot wait for cupcakes and candy and games. But that day all I could think about was whether Ricky had put a valentine in my mailbox. I did not think he had. If that were true, I would just *die*.

"Party time!" said Ms. Colman.

"Yea!" cried everyone except me.

Mrs. Papadakis was one of the room mothers. She placed a pink frosted cupcake on everyone's desk. Bobby Gianelli's mom was the other room mother. She passed out red hots and punch. We were allowed to talk while we ate. I wished I could talk to Hannie and Nancy, but they were too far away.

I turned around in my seat anyway to look at the rest of the class. That was when it happened. The awful thing.

Pamela said loudly, "Hey, Ricky!"

"Yeah?" Ricky turned around in his seat, too.

"Happy Valentine's Day!" said Pamela. Then she looked at me.

Ricky blushed. "Happy Valentine's Day," he murmured.

I tried to ignore Pamela. I ate my food. I ate the red hots, one by one. Then I drank half of my punch. Then I peeled the wrapper off of my cupcake. Then I ate all the icing off the top. (Icing is really the only good part of a cupcake.) Then I ate the rest of the cupcake, too. And then I finished my punch.

After we had eaten our snack, Ms. Colman said it was time for games. First we played one sitting in our seats. Ms. Colman wrote VALENTINE on the board. We were supposed to see how many words we could make from the letters in "valentine."

I found fifteen words. (This was a hard game.) I won the game, though! (Well, I tied with Natalie, who also found fifteen words.)

After that game, Ms. Colman organized a Heart Race. It was a sort of relay race with paper hearts. I played the game as well as I could. But my heart was not in it. (Get it? My *heart* was not in it?)

All I could think of was my mailbox. It looked full. But there was only one valentine card I *really* cared about. (You know who that was from.)

He loves me, he loves me not, I thought.

# 2 Good 2 B 4-Gotten

"All right, class," said Ms. Colman. "Everybody back to your desks."

The relay race was over. Pamela's team had won. (Of course.)

"You may now," said Ms. Colman, "see what's inside your mailboxes."

In a flash, everyone pulled the valentine pouches off of their desks. I emptied mine out. A pile of cards fell in front of me. One of them *must* be from Ricky!

I looked around to see how many cards

other people had gotten. Most had gotten about the same as me.

Guess who had gotten more than anyone else. Pamela.

Guess who got the least. Natalie.

Natalie's eyes were red. I hoped she wouldn't start to cry. When she cries she snorts, and I did not want snorting at the party.

Okay, here goes, I thought, as I reached for my first card. I ripped it open. It was from Natalie.

"Hey, Natalie! Thanks!" I called. I waved the card in the air. It was a Snoopy card. Natalie gave me a tiny smile.

I opened card after card. I got cards from Hannie, Nancy, the twins, and Hank Reubens. I got two cards that were not signed. At last there was only one card left. It did not look special. It was just an ordinary card.

But it *had* to be from Ricky. It just *had* to be.

I opened it. It was from a girl named Audrey.

I could not help what happened next. Tears filled my eyes. I did not want to cry in front of my whole class. (But if I did, at least I would not snort.)

All of a sudden, an envelope was dropped on my desk. I looked up. Ms. Colman had put it there. I opened it in a big hurry.

It said: "To Karen, a shining star. Happy Valentine's Day! From Ms. Colman."

That was nice. I would always keep the card. But what I really wanted was a card from Ricky. One tear rolled down my cheek. I wiped it away. Then I looked over at Ricky. He was opening *my* card! Oh. . . .

Ricky stared at the valentine for a long time. Then he glanced at me. A funny look was on his face. I was gigundo worried.

Ricky reached inside his desk. He pulled out a huge envelope. And he handed it to *me*. Very carefully, I opened it. I pulled out a beautiful card. Ricky had bought it at a store. On the outside were hearts and flowers and butterflies and birds. On the inside Ricky had written: "I'm sorry about our fight. Will you still marry me? Love, Ricky. (U R 2 good 2 B 4-gotten.)"

"Ricky!" I exclaimed. "You mean you aren't mad anymore?"

"No. Are you?"

"No. Is the wedding on? Are we going to get married?"

"Sure," replied Ricky. "How about Monday? On the playground? That way everyone can come."

"Everyone who *wants* to," I said. I was thinking that Pamela would not show up.

I ran to the back of the room. I waved Ricky's valentine in the air.

"Ricky and I are getting married on Monday on the playground," I told Hannie and Nancy. "Spread it around."

"Congratulations!" cried Nancy.

She and Hannie ran off with the news.

By the time the bell had rung and the

party was over, everyone in our class knew about the wedding. *Most* of them were excited.

Not Natalie Springer, though. She just looked sad. And I knew why. It was because of her valentines. It must feel awful to get just a few cards when everyone else gets a lot. I would have to think of something nice to do for Natalie.

# 15

# Santa Claus Sam

The next day I woke up in my big-house bedroom. Moosie and Tickly were by my side. I smiled. I had a lot to look forward to. First would be our big-house valentine party. Then I would get Hannie to help me with plans for the wedding. And on Monday . . . Ricky and I would get married!

I leaped out of bed. I was excited about our party. It would be a special morning party. Afterward, we would go out to lunch at McDonald's. It would be Emily's first time there. Can you believe that she had never been to a McDonald's?

At eleven o'clock that morning I heard Daddy calling around the house, "Party time! Party time! Everyone report to the living room immediately!"

Daddy can be so silly.

I grabbed my valentines and ran downstairs to the living room. Soon my whole big-house family was there. We were holding cards, and *Sam* had a pile of gifts with him. They were gigundo pretty — all wrapped in red paper and tied with white ribbon.

I was so excited that I shouted, "Everyone, hand out your valentines!" (Nobody bothered to tell me to use my indoor voice. I guess they were as excited as I was.)

So we passed out our cards. Sam passed out his cards and gifts. Everyone began opening everything at once. Except for Emily. Emily did not understand cards and Valentine's Day. So Daddy and Elizabeth opened her things for her. They kept pointing to pictures on the cards and telling her what they were. Finally, Emily learned a new word: heart. Only she pronounced it "hot."

I noticed that everyone was opening their cards first and saving Sam's presents for last. So I did the same thing. (I felt bad that I did not have a present for Sam.)

Nannie's card to me was sweet. It was the flowery kind.

David Michael's card had a joke on it:

"Why did the chicken cross the playground?
To get to the other slide!"

Finally there was nothing left to open except Sam's presents. Emily Michelle looked from Sam to the presents and back to Sam. Then she asked, "Santa?"

Everyone laughed.

We opened Sam's boxes. Guess what was in mine. Nothing! Guess what was in

Kristy's. Cotton balls! Guess what was in Nannie's. One red hot candy! All of Sam's presents were like that. (I stopped feeling bad about not having a present for him.)

When everything had been opened, we piled into two cars for our trip to McDonald's.

"Yum," I said as soon as we stepped inside. "I know what I'm going to order. A cheeseburger, French fries, and a vanilla milkshake."

"*I'm* going to have *two* hamburgers, a large order of French fries, and a large soda," said Charlie. (Charlie can eat an awful lot.)

"Soda?" spoke up Emily. "Soda?"

"You can have a soda," Elizabeth told her.

But Emily was running off. She had spotted a huge clown across the restaurant. (It was not a real one.) Daddy ran after her. He caught up with her just as Emily reached the clown. "Ronald McDonald!" said Emily very clearly.

Soon we had our food. We sat down in booths. We took up three! David Michael and Andrew and I were allowed to sit by ourselves. We felt very grown-up.

Daddy and Elizabeth sat with Emily. Emily was excited by everything. She opened up packages of catsup and salt. She pulled napkins out of the holder. She kept saying, "Ronald McDonald!" But she did not eat a thing.

McDonald's was fun. All I could think about, though, was going home and planning my wedding with Hannie.

# Wedding Plans

I was out of the car almost before Daddy had parked it. I ran inside the big house to hog the telephone. I needed to call Hannie right away. Since she was married, she was a wedding expert. And we had to plan a whole wedding by Monday.

"Hello, Hannie?" I said, when she answered the phone.

"Karen?"

"It's me! Hi! Can you come over right away? We have to plan my wedding."

Hannie said she would be there. In about five minutes the doorbell rang.

I answered it. Hannie and I ran upstairs to my room. We closed the door. We needed privacy. Then we sat on my bed. We both looked serious. (Well, this *was* serious business.)

"There is so much to talk about," I began. "Where should we start?"

"Your dress," said Hannie. "It has to be just right." Hannie sounded very professional.

"It won't show much," I reminded her. "We're getting married outdoors. It's cold. I'll have my coat on."

"But Ricky will see you in school. So you'll want to look nice, won't you?"

"Definitely."

"Okay, let's see," said Hannie.

"I'll be getting dressed at Mommy's," I reminded Hannie. "So it has to be a little-house outfit." I thought for a moment. "What about the dress with the tiny flowers all over it, and the lacy collar? Mommy will probably let me wear my party shoes, too."

"That sounds fine. And can you wear your good coat?"

"I think so," I replied.

"Terrific. Now what about flowers? Since it's winter you can't pick any. You'll have to buy them."

"I don't think I have enough money for that," I replied. . . . "Hey! How about paper flowers? That would be so, so special. You know why?"

"No. Why?" asked Hannie.

"Because when Ricky asked me to marry him, he gave me a paper flower."

"Perfect!" said Hannie.

"There's just one problem," I went on. "Actually, there are three problems: Pamela, Jannie, and Leslie. I know that Ricky and I decided to invite our whole class, but I'm worried that Pamela and her friends will come to the wedding and ruin it. Or laugh at us."

"Maybe you can un-invite them," suggested Hannie.

"I don't think that would do any good. It's a free playground. They'd just come anyway," I said. "Maybe we could tell Pamela that the wedding was changed to Tuesday. Then we'll hold it Monday, someplace where they won't see us."

"That sounds sort of complicated, Karen."

"I know. I guess we'll just stick to our old plan."

"Maybe Pamela won't want to come to the wedding," said Hannie.

"I hope not. But maybe she will. And maybe she'll make everyone laugh or something."

"Or maybe she'll come and behave herself."

"I don't know. She likes Ricky. I think she's jealous that he's marrying me."

Finally, Hannie and I decided just to hope that Pamela would not show up.

Then we started making paper flowers.

"Weddings take *lots* of flowers," said Hannie wisely.

So we made a bouquet for me to carry.

(The stems of the flowers were pipe cleaners.) We made a flower to pin to Ricky's jacket. And then we made a lot of other flowers.

When we were finished, Hannie had to go home.

# 17

# Bridesmaids and Violins

After Hannie left, I realized I had a lot more planning to do. We had made flowers. We had chosen my outfit. But I still needed bridesmaids. (I would ask Hannie and Nancy, of course.) And Ricky needed . . . bridesmen? I was not sure what they were called. But he would need some boys to stand next to him while we were getting married. And he needed the same number of boys as bridesmaids.

We also needed music. Plus, I had to make sure that Ricky would wear a suit.

84

And I had to make sure that Ricky had a ring for me. (I had found one for him. It was very beautiful. I had gotten it out of a gumball machine.)

Plus, we needed someone to marry Ricky and me.

I decided to call Ricky. If he was going to be my husband, he should help make these decisions. We should be a team.

"Ricky," I said when he got on the phone, "I need to talk to you."

I must have sounded very serious, because Ricky said, "You don't want to get married after all, do you."

"Oh, no! It's not that," I exclaimed. "Of course I want to marry you! But we have plans to make. Hannie and I already decided what I should wear. And we figured out the flowers. But you and I need to talk about some other things."

"Like what?"

"Like what *you're* going to wear. I will be very dressed up. So you should wear a suit."

Ricky sighed.

"And you need to choose two . . . I forget what they're called. But I've decided to ask Hannie and Nancy to be my bridesmaids, so you need — "

"Two ushers," supplied Ricky. "Okay, I'll have to think. But I promise to have two ushers by Monday."

"Great," I said. "And they have to wear suits, too."

Ricky sighed again. "This is almost as bad as school-picture day."

I ignored what Ricky had said.

"We also need someone to marry us," I went on.

Ricky and I talked about that. At last we decided that Audrey would be good for the job.

"Um," I began, "there's another thing. When people get married, they give each other rings. I have a ring for you, but . . ."

Ricky laughed. "Don't worry," he said. "I have a ring for you, too."

Whew!

"The last thing we need is music," I told Ricky.

"Can you take care of that?" he asked me. "I don't know much about music."

"Sure," I replied. "I'll figure something out."

After Ricky and I got off the phone, I thought and thought. Music. I could bring a radio to school. But maybe we would not be able to find a good station during the ceremony. Maybe we could — I was in the middle of a thought when I got a really great idea. One of my best ideas ever.

I picked up the phone. "Hello," I said when someone answered. "Is Natalie there?"

A few moments later I heard Natalie's voice say, "Hello?"

"Hi," I said. "It's me, Karen Brewer. I have something to ask you."

"What?" said Natalie.

"Well, you know that Ricky and I are getting married on Monday. And we need music at the wedding. I was wondering if you would play your violin."

"*Me?*" squeaked Natalie. "You want *me* to play at your wedding?"

"Yes," I replied. I was pleased that Natalie sounded happy. I wanted her to feel better.

"I've only taken a few lessons," Natalie warned me. "All I can play is 'Twinkle, Twinkle, Little Star.'"

I thought for a moment. Finally I said, "That will be just fine."

Then I called Hannie and Nancy. They both said they would be my bridesmaids. They even have matching dresses. They would wear them on Monday so they would look alike.

The wedding was all set!

# 18

## "Nah, Nah, Nah-Nah, Nah!"

Monday was wedding day.

I was gigundo nervous. I don't think I've ever been so nervous. Not even the time when I was in a spelling bee and I got to go on television.

I peeked out the window. Since the wedding would be held outdoors, I was hoping for nice weather. Yea! The sun was out. And it had not rained over the weekend, so the playground would be dry. (Sometimes it is muddy.) Maybe the air would even warm up a little.

I have always wanted a spring wedding.
Oh, well. The nice weather cheered me up. I did not feel so nervous. And I did not care that I was getting married in February.

Just as Hannie and I planned, I put on my flowery dress. Mommy let me wear my good coat. Also my party shoes. But she put my rubber boots in a paper bag. She made me bring the bag to school. "If it begins to rain," she said, "then you'll have to wear your boots. I don't want those shoes to get wet."

"Okay," I promised.

When I reached school, I saw Ricky first thing. He had remembered to wear his suit. And somehow he had made Hank Reubens and Bobby Gianelli wear suits, too. They were going to be the ushers. Hannie and Nancy were wearing their matching dresses. They looked very wonderful.

More and more kids came into the room. Most of them were dressed up, too. I was

pleased. The wedding was important to them.

Audrey was wearing a blue dress. "My mother usually only lets me wear this to church," she told me.

Natalie was wearing a pink jumper over a lacy white blouse. Her socks were falling down, but who cared?

The twins were dressed up, too. In fact, so was everybody except for Pamela, Leslie, and Jannie. They were wearing blue jeans and sweat shirts.

Good, I thought. That means they are not coming to the wedding.

Wrong.

Before Ms. Colman started class, Pamela wandered over to my desk.

"I guess today is the big day," she said.

"Yup," I replied.

"I got all dressed up for the wedding. So did Leslie and Jannie."

"You call that dressed up?" I said.

"It's as dressed up as you got for my birthday party," replied Pamela.

I did not answer her.

Later that morning, Ms. Colman had to go down the hall to the supply room. She left Nancy in charge of our class. Nancy got to sit at Ms. Colman's desk.

As soon as Ms. Colman had gone, Leslie began to sing, *"Karen's getting married. Karen's getting married."*

Jannie joined her. Then Pamela did, too.

"You guys are just jealous," I whispered, turning around in my seat.

From Ms. Colman's desk, Nancy clapped her hands. "Quiet, please!"

"Oh, you just think you're so great because you're in Karen and Ricky's wedding," Pamela said to Nancy. "I hope you know you look pretty stupid dressed the same as Hannie. Even Terri and Tammy don't dress alike."

"Sometimes we dress alike," said Terri haughtily.

"SHH!" hissed Nancy. "Here comes Ms. Colman."

I stuck out my tongue at Pamela. Then I went back to my work.

"*Nah, nah, nah-nah, nah!*" sang Pamela just before Ms. Colman walked into the room.

# 19

## Kiss! Kiss!

Finally the morning was over. It was time for lunch, and then time for recess. As I walked onto the playground with Hannie and Nancy, I was not sure I should have eaten such a big lunch. I was even more nervous now than I had been before. Oh, well. It was too late.

At least it was not raining. I would not have to get married in rubber boots.

The people in the wedding — Nancy, Hannie, Bobby, Hank, Natalie, and Audrey — gathered around Ricky and me.

"Where are we going to have the wedding?" asked Audrey.

I looked all around the playground. At last I said, "Over there." I pointed to an area that was far away from swings and slides and dodgeball games. Then I turned to Ricky. "Is that all right with you?" I asked.

"It's fine," Ricky replied. He looked a little uncomfortable, though.

I wanted to ask him what was wrong, but everyone was walking to the place I had pointed to. And we were being followed by a lot of wedding guests.

When we reached the spot, I turned to Hannie. "Do you have the flowers?" I whispered? (I had given Hannie the paper flowers that morning. She was in charge of them.)

"Yup," she replied, and she passed out a flower to everyone who was in the wedding. I had put a piece of rolled-up Scotch tape on the back of each flower so that everyone could stick them to their coats.

"Okay," I said. "Now, Audrey, you are going to marry us. So you stand here. Pretend you're standing at the end of a long aisle. Hannie and Nancy, you stand next to Audrey. Bobby and Hank, you stand next to Audrey, too, but on her other side. Now all you guests, you stand on one side or the other, and leave a path for Ricky and me to walk down. All right?"

The kids separated into two groups.

Uh-oh. At the back of one group were Pamela, Jannie, and Leslie. I had been hoping they would decide not to come. Well, if they did anything, I would ignore them. That was all there was to it.

"Okay, Natalie," I said.

Natalie put her violin up to her chin. *"Twinkle, twinkle, little star . . ."*

Ricky and I linked arms. We walked toward Audrey. Everybody was very quiet. Except for Natalie. She was not only playing her violin. She was crying — and snorting.

I turned around to look at her. What was wrong?

"Don't worry," said Natalie, snorting again. "These are tears of happiness." She went back to "Twinkle, Twinkle, Little Star."

So Ricky and I kept on walking. We walked to Audrey and stood in front of her.

Audrey began a long speech. She said things about loving forever, and not fighting, and cherishing each other. *Finally*, she said, "Okay, exchange rings."

I pulled the ring for Ricky out of the pocket of my coat. But Ricky just stood there. He looked more uncomfortable than ever. Finally, he whispered to me, "I forgot your ring."

I thought quickly. Then I slid my plastic spider ring off of my finger. I slipped it to Ricky. "Here," I said. "Give this to me for now."

So Ricky put the spider ring back on my finger, and then I gave him his ring.

"I now pronounce you husband and wife," said Audrey. She looked at Ricky. "You may kiss Karen."

"Kiss! Kiss!" chanted the crowd of kids.

Ricky's face grew red. And while I was waiting for him to kiss me, I guess Bobby Gianelli got sort of carried away by things. He leaned over to Pamela, who was now standing next to him — and he kissed her cheek!

"Gross!" shrieked Pamela.

And at that moment, Ricky leaned toward *me*.

# 20

# Karen the Bride

Did I want to be kissed? I wondered. Pamela had screamed, "Gross!" when Bobby kissed her. However, Pamela does not like Bobby.

Ricky was coming closer and closer. And then . . . I could feel his kiss on my cheek.

Ooh. Suddenly I knew how love *really* feels. And I was in love for sure. I looked at Ricky, wide-eyed.

"We're married," I whispered.

"I guess so." Ricky's face was still red.

The bell rang then, so our wedding had to be over. My classmates ran to line up.

Ricky and I did not run with them. I am not sure how Ricky felt, but I was quite pleased. (Also, I was in love.) We linked arms again and we walked toward the school building.

I could not believe it. I was married, just like Hannie.

I was a wife.

Ricky was my husband.

Ricky and I were the last kids to enter our class. Everyone stared at us. Most of our friends were smiling.

Hank called out, "Whoo! Ricky is in lo-ove!"

Ricky?! What about me? I was in love, too.

I loved being in love.

"Okay, class," said Ms. Colman as we were taking our seats. "Please find your spelling books. Then choose a partner. I would like you to quiz each other on the words on page forty-two."

Well, of course, Ricky and I had to be partners.

We opened our books to page forty-two.

I looked at my husband. "Spell 'important,' " I said.

And Ricky replied, "Hey!" But he did not say it too loudly. I guess he didn't want Ms. Colman to hear him.

"What?" I asked.

Ricky held out his hand. In it was a ring. It was gold with a big blue stone. It looked just like the rings the dentist gives me when I don't have any cavities.

"Here's your ring," Ricky whispered. "I thought I left it at home, but it's right here in my desk. Should I put it on your finger?"

I checked to see if Ms. Colman was watching. She wasn't. She was writing something on the blackboard. (The blackboard is green, by the way.)

"Yes," I whispered to Ricky.

I switched my spider ring to another finger. Then I held out my left hand. Ricky

103

put the ring with the blue stone on my wedding finger.

*Now* we were officially married.

We looked at our spelling books. I started over. " 'Important,' " I said to Ricky.

Ricky spelled it almost right. He spelled it I-M-P-O-R-T-E-N-T. Then he gave me a word to spell. After that we kept switching off.

Even though I spelled all of my words correctly, I was not really thinking about spelling. I was thinking about something else.

I was thinking about my last name. When Mommy married Daddy, she changed her last name to Brewer. When she married Seth, she changed her last name to Engle.

Should I change my last name to Torres? Did I want to be Karen Torres? Or maybe I could combine our names. I could be Karen Torres-Brewer. Or Karen Brewer-Torres.

I thought and thought. Finally I made a decision.

I was, and always will be, Karen Brewer.

## About the Author

ANN M. MARTIN lives in New York City and loves animals. Her cat, Mouse, knows how to take the phone off the hook.

Other books by Ann M. Martin that you might enjoy are *Stage Fright*, *Me and Katie (the Pest)*, and the books in *The Baby-sitters Club* series.

Ann likes ice cream, the beach, and *I Love Lucy*. And she has her own little sister, whose name is Jane.

## Little Sister

Don't miss #16

### KAREN'S GOLDFISH

Andrew and I tore upstairs to the play-room. We had to decide what kind of pet to get.

"A snake," said Andrew, as soon as we were sitting on the floor.

"No way," I replied.

"How about a frog or a turtle?"

"No. No gross green things. Let's get a guinea pig. Or a gerbil."

"But you already have a rat at Mommy's. That's sort of the same."

"Well, we're *not* getting a snake."

"But I *want* one!" cried Andrew.

"But getting a big-house pet was my idea," I pointed out. "So — Hey, I know! How about a fish? They're *really* small."

"A goldfishie?" said Andrew.

"Whatever. A fish is perfect. Maybe Daddy would even let us get two."

"Yeah!" exclaimed Andrew.

# You Can Be the Lucky BIRTHDAY KID!

## Join the

# BABY-SITTERS

## Little Sister

# Birthday Club!

Happy Birthday to you! Join the **Baby-sitters Little Sister Birthday Club** and on your birthday, you'll receive a personalized card from Karen herself!

That's not all! Every month, a **BIRTHDAY KID OF THE MONTH** will be randomly chosen to **WIN** a complete set of *Baby-sitters Little Sister* books! The set's first book will be autographed by author Ann M. Martin!

Just fill in the coupon below. Offer expires March 31, 1992. Fill in the coupon below or write the information on a 3" x 5" piece of paper and mail to: BABY-SITTERS LITTLE SISTER BIRTHDAY CLUB, Scholastic Inc., 730 Broadway, P.O. Box 742, New York, New York 10003.

----

## *Baby-sitters Little Sister* Birthday Club

❏ **YES!** I want to join the BABY-SITTERS LITTLE SISTER BIRTHDAY CLUB!

My birthday is _____

Name _____ Age _____

Street _____

City _____ State _____ Zip _____

**P.S.** Please put your birthday on the outside of your envelope too! Thanks!

### Where did you buy this *Baby-sitters Little Sister* book?

❏ Bookstore     ❏ Drugstore     ❏ Supermarket     ❏ Library
❏ Book Club     ❏ Book Fair     ❏ Other_____(specify)

BLS890